THE PUZZLE CLUB™

CHRISTMAS MYSTERY

ADAPTED BY DANDI DALEY MACKALL

ILLUSTRATED BY MIKE YOUNG PRODUCTIONS

BASED ON *THE PUZZLE CLUB CHRISTMAS MYSTERY*
ORIGINAL STORY BY MARK YOUNG
FOR LUTHERAN HOUR MINISTRIES

CPH.
SAINT LOUIS

Lutheran Hour
Ministries

W ith two days till Christmas, the whole town should have been celebrating. Instead, disappointment and sadness were spoiling the Christmas spirit. And no one was sadder than little Michelle Pennington.

Real shame about the parade, eh?" Rafferty said, ripping down another parade poster.

"The sheriff'll find that thief Pennington and slap him in jail!" said Lucas. "Why, taking our money and skipping town, that's like stealing the Christmas parade."

M ichelle called out to Lucas. "He didn't steal the money!" she screamed. "Honest! You have to believe me."

Michelle's mother took her daughter's hand and tugged her away.

Alex, junior detective of The Puzzle Club, had big news. He burst into Puzzleworks. "Tobias!"

Poor old Tobias bumped into his puzzle Christmas tree. Puzzle pieces crashed to the floor.

"Oops," said Alex. "Sorry, Tobias."

The old man chuckled. "Merry Christmas, Alex," he said.

Tobias pulled a gold cord. A shelf of games slid to the side, revealing a secret stairway to Puzzle Club headquarters.

Alex flew up the stairs. "Christopher! Korina!" he shouted. "Wait till you hear! I've got my own terrific mystery!"

Korina looked doubtful. "We already know about Pennington running away with the parade money, Alex," she said. She looked down at the angel costume she was wearing. "I won't need this anymore."

"Not *that* mystery," Alex said. "*My* mystery."

Chills ran down Alex's spine as he told what happened that morning on the Bascomb Road shortcut ...

"And in the creepiest old house I saw ... really saw ... I *know* I saw ... A WEIRD, SCARY SHAPE!"

*B*raawk! *Scary shape!*" Sherlock the parakeet buried his face in Alex's sweatshirt.

"Real lame, Alex," Korina said.

"That's your mystery?" asked Christopher, the leader of The Puzzle Club.

But Alex convinced them to investigate *The Case of Alex's Weird and Scary Shape.*

Twenty years ago Bascomb Road was a rich neighborhood. Now The Puzzle Club biked past deserted houses, broken bottles, and empty lots.

"aybe it's a ghost," Christopher said. "Bascomb Mansion sure looks haunted." Christopher took pictures while Korina and Alex examined the weedy yard.

Alex was trying to get up nerve to go inside when he saw something in a window. There was his ghost—only now it was *glowing!*

Christopher led The Puzzle Club charge to capture the Bascomb Mansion ghost. But the glowing shape had vanished, leaving only two clues. A crumpled necktie and a handful of hay.

he next day, as The Puzzle Club raced to headquarters to analyze the clues, they were stopped by a crowd in the town square. Sherrif Grimaldi was interviewing Rafferty.

"Someone stole the nativity!" Rafferty exclaimed.

Sure enough. All that was left was the manger ... and the figure of baby Jesus.

The next day at headquarters, Alex felt sure his Bascomb Mansion ghost was responsible for the disappearing nativity figures.

While Christopher developed his photos, Korina argued with Alex. "You're jumping to conclusions again, Alex."

Suddenly The Puzzle Club door swung open, scaring Alex and Sherlock. Tobias stepped in with little Michelle at his side.

"Please," she said. "I need you to solve a mystery for me."

A lex started to explain that they already had a mystery when Michelle grabbed the crumpled tie off the table. "It's my daddy's tie!" she cried. "Your ghost must have taken him too!"

Y ou have to find my dad by six o'clock tonight," Michelle pleaded. "My parents had an argument. My mom packed our bags. I think we're leaving town forever."

The Puzzle Club decided to take Michelle's case … until she gave them her full name: Michelle *Pennington*.

Alex shut his notebook. "Your dad disappeared with our parade money!" he said.

We can't help someone who's done such an unforgivable thing," said Korina.

"Alex, Korina," Christopher said, "Michelle needs our help."

"Think how you'd feel losing your father," Tobias said.

Alex thought about how awful that would be. He glanced at Korina. She nodded. "We'll take the case!" he said.

This time Tobias went with The Puzzle Club to Bascomb Road. Christopher shined his flashlight into the old mansion kitchen. Empty cans and trash littered the floor.

"Looks like Alex's ghost eats pretty well," said Christopher.

lex tiptoed down the hall and tried the dining room door. Slowly it opened. A huge creature seemed to lunge out at him! Alex ran, screaming down the hall. "A monster! Pointy fangs! Huge claws!"

hat cow does look pretty dangerous, Alex," teased Korina.

Alex's monster turned out to be nothing more than one of the missing animals from the town nativity scene. In the middle of the dining room, all neatly arranged, stood the stolen figures from the nativity.

The doorknob on the basement door slowly turned. Christopher herded the others into a closet to hide. Alex's heart pounded as they waited. A weird, scary shape moved down the hall.

"Now!" cried Christopher. And The Puzzle Club fell out of the closet in front of the Bascomb Mansion ghost!

I t's Todd Pennington!" Tobias exclaimed, as Michelle's dad made a getaway.

"Wait!" Christopher said. "Your daughter sent us."

That stopped Pennington in his tracks. "My poor Michelle," he said. "And my poor wife."

Then Michelle's dad told them everything—how he'd given the parade money to the carnival man who had run off with it. "I was afraid nobody would believe me. The pressure got to me. I was putting up our nativity when I exploded at my wife. I said terrible things ... unforgivable things. I miss my family. And I miss Christmas. That's why I took the nativity figures."

Alex felt sorry for Michelle's dad. "I don't understand, Mr. Pennington," he said. "You took the nativity figures, but you left the baby Jesus," he said. "What's Christmas without Jesus?"

Christopher put a hand on Pennington's arm. "God loves you," he said. "Christmas is about God sending His Son, Jesus, into our crazy world." But Todd Pennington's shoulders still slumped with the weight of his guilt.

Alex stepped up. "God understands that we can mess things up pretty badly."

"He gave up His Son's life to bring us forgiveness," Korina added.

Tobias smiled so warmly *he* almost glowed. "The kids are saying that forgiveness through Jesus gives you a fresh start."

Todd Pennington straightened up, his face shining with hope. "You mean it's *not* too late for a fresh start?" he cried.

"*Braawk!*" screeched Sherlock. "*Fresh start!*"

"But we have to get you home," said Christopher. "In a few minutes, your family is leaving town ... forever!"

obias drove the kids to Pennington's house, but they were too late. Just as the van pulled up to the curb, a taxi drove off—with Michelle and her mother inside. Todd Pennington ran after the taxi, waving his arms wildly, but the cab kept going.

"I'm so sorry," Pennington said. "I can't have a fresh start after what I've done. I'm so sorry."

Braawk!*" Sherlock pointed to something in the distance. A taxi cab
… coming toward them!

The door opened and Carol Pennington ran into the arms of her
husband.

Todd hugged his wife and daughter. "Please forgive me," he said. "This
will be the best Christmas ever. Our fresh start."

 hristmas morning a crowd gathered around the nativity. "I was
wrong about Todd Pennington," Rafferty said. "Sherrif said he's got some
leads on that carnival thief. Give me a hand with this nativity?"

Alex couldn't have been happier. Not only were both Christmas
mysteries solved, but Christopher and Korina made him a full member of
The Puzzle Club.

Michelle and her mother watched as Todd Pennington gently placed the figure of baby Jesus in the manger. He thought of the real baby who had come to be his Savior. "Thank You," he whispered, "for the hope of my fresh start."